THE VIKING

CHILDREN'S WORLD ATLAS

An Introductory Atlas for Young People

Jacqueline Tivers and Michael Day

The Viking Press/New York

Published in 1983 by The Viking Press
40 West 23rd Street, New York, New York 10010

Published simultaneously in Canada by Penguin Books Canada Limited

Printed in Great Britain   4   5   87   86   85

Library of Congress Cataloging in Publication Data
Tivers, Jacqueline.
    The Viking children's world atlas.

    Summary: An introductory atlas taking the reader from
the home to solar system.
    1. Atlases Juvenile literature. (Atlases)   I. Day, Michael, 1983
    II. The Viking Press.   II. Title.
G1021.T583   1983   912   83-675053
ISBN 0-670-21791-3

Acknowledgements

The publishers wish to thank Robert Harding Associates, Colour
Library International, Spectrum Colour Library, British
Petroleum, C. Peter Kimber, Pica Design, Laurence R. Lowry/
Louis Mercier, and David Muench for providing photographs
for use in this edition.

Contents

Introducing Simon and Sarah

Simon and Sarah are going to visit many countries and find lots of interesting places to tell you about.

This is Simon   and this is Sarah

Simon and Sarah live in this house.

Their house is on a street with other houses. This is a simple map of the street. The red square is their house.

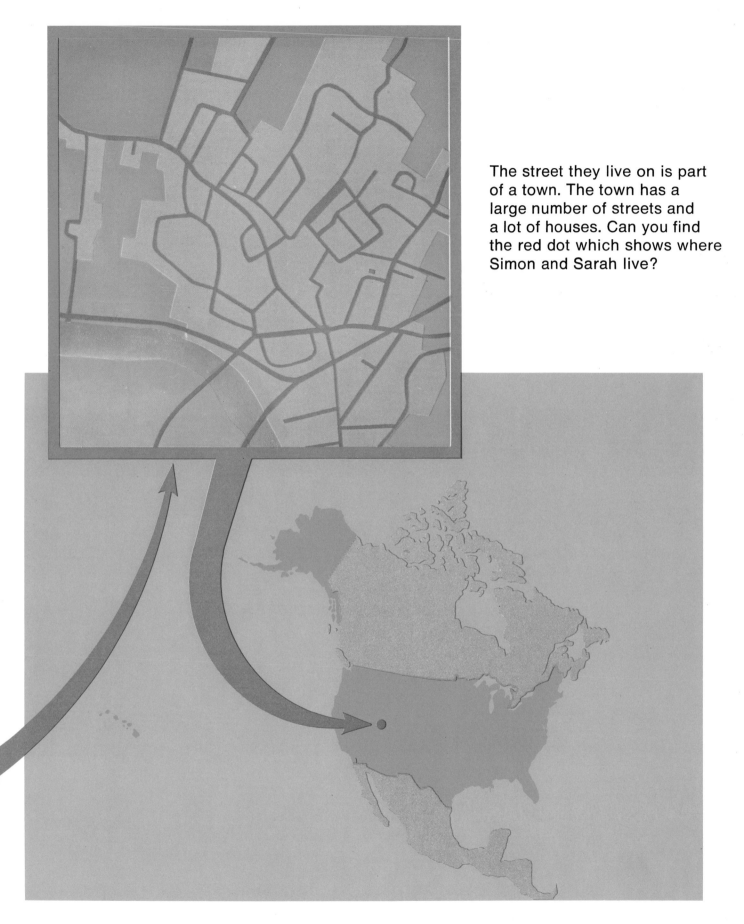

The street they live on is part of a town. The town has a large number of streets and a lot of houses. Can you find the red dot which shows where Simon and Sarah live?

Their town is in the United States, which is a large country. The red dot shows where the town is on this map. As you can see on the map, the United States goes from one ocean to the other. It also has two other parts. The state of Alaska is in the far North. The state of Hawaii is far out in the Pacific Ocean. Can you find the United States on the map on pages 6 and 7? On pages 10, 11, 12, and 13 there are bigger maps of the United States.

World Map

On this map of the world, we can see the country where Simon and Sarah live. The United States is shaded in red.

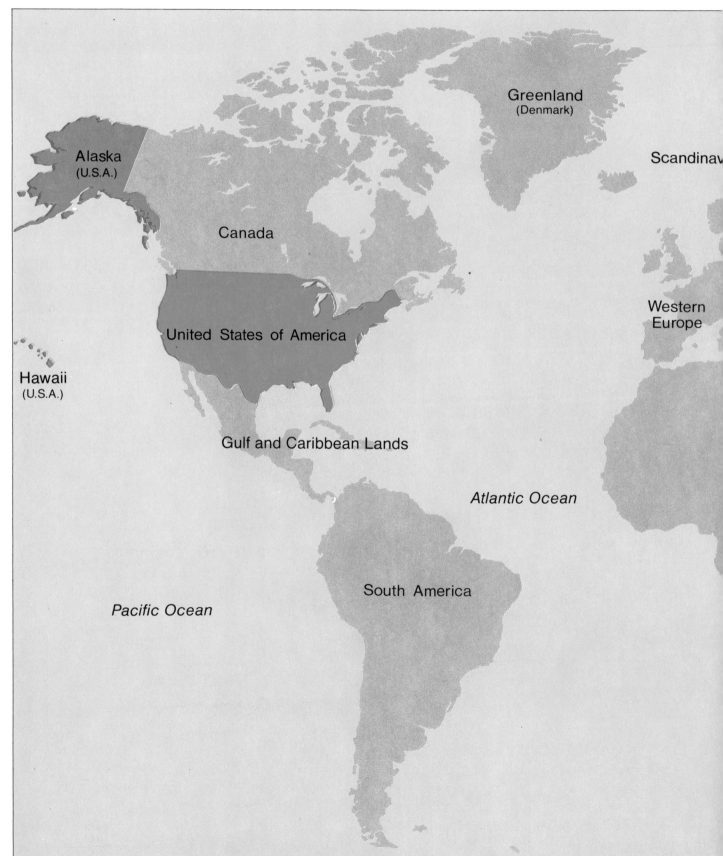

Greenland
(Denmark)

Scandinav

Alaska
(U.S.A.)

Canada

Western
Europe

United States of America

Hawaii
(U.S.A.)

Gulf and Caribbean Lands

Atlantic Ocean

South America

Pacific Ocean

Each part of the world that Simon and Sarah are going to visit is shown, too.

On every page of the book you will find a small map of the world. It shows in red the area that Simon and Sarah are visiting.

Arctic Ocean

Soviet Union

astern
urope

China and Its Neighbors

Japan

Middle East

South-West Asia

Pacific Ocean

Africa

South-East Asia

Indian Ocean

Australia

New Zealand

Of course, the continents of the world are not really blank as they appear on the last map. Some parts of the world are covered with thick forests. Other parts are desert or farmland. In some areas there are high mountains and deep valleys. As Simon and Sarah travel around the world they will see all these different types of land, and the maps of the places they visit will be shaded in different colors.

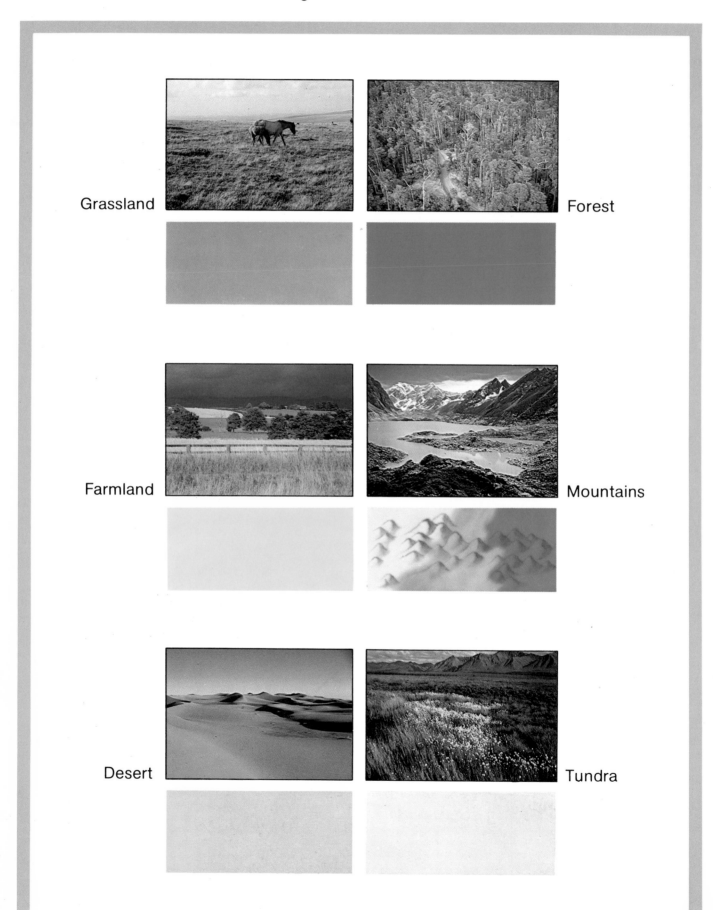

Grassland

Forest

Farmland

Mountains

Desert

Tundra

Simon and Sarah will also see some of the things people do in the countries they visit. The symbols on the maps will show where people work, the crops they grow, and the animals they keep.

These are the symbols you will find on the maps.

The crops people grow

 timber

 wheat and barley

 corn

 rice

 potatoes and yams

 peanuts or groundnuts

 apples and pears

 oranges and lemons

 grapes

 bananas

 dates

 sugar

 coffee

 tea

 cocoa

 cotton

 rubber

 tobacco

 palm oil

The animals people keep

 cows (Europe and America)

 cows (Africa and Asia)

 sheep (Europe and Australia)

 sheep (Africa and Asia)

 pigs

Where people work

 offices

 factories

 mining

 coal mining

 oil and gas

 nuclear power

 sea port

 fishing port

Places for holidays

 beach vacations

 skiing vacations

 hiking vacations

Look for Simon and Sarah on every map and see what they are doing in each part of the world.

On most pages you will also find some wild animal symbols, such as lions, birds, and elephants. These show where those animals live.

United States of America

Indian tribes once wandered freely all over what is now called the United States. Then other people came to live in America from many different parts of the world. Today the United States has modern farms, small towns, big cities, and many different kinds of industry.

Many cities have tall buildings, called skyscrapers, where people work in offices. The buildings are tall because land in the cities costs a lot of money. It is cheaper to build upwards than outwards. This map shows the continental United States. On pages 12 and 13 there is a map of all the states.

Missouri

Denver

Colorado

Grand Canyon

San Francisco

Los Angeles

Many visitors come to see the Grand Canyon. A river runs through the deep, winding gorge.

In this field, corn is being harvested. The corn is stored in the round buildings, called silos.

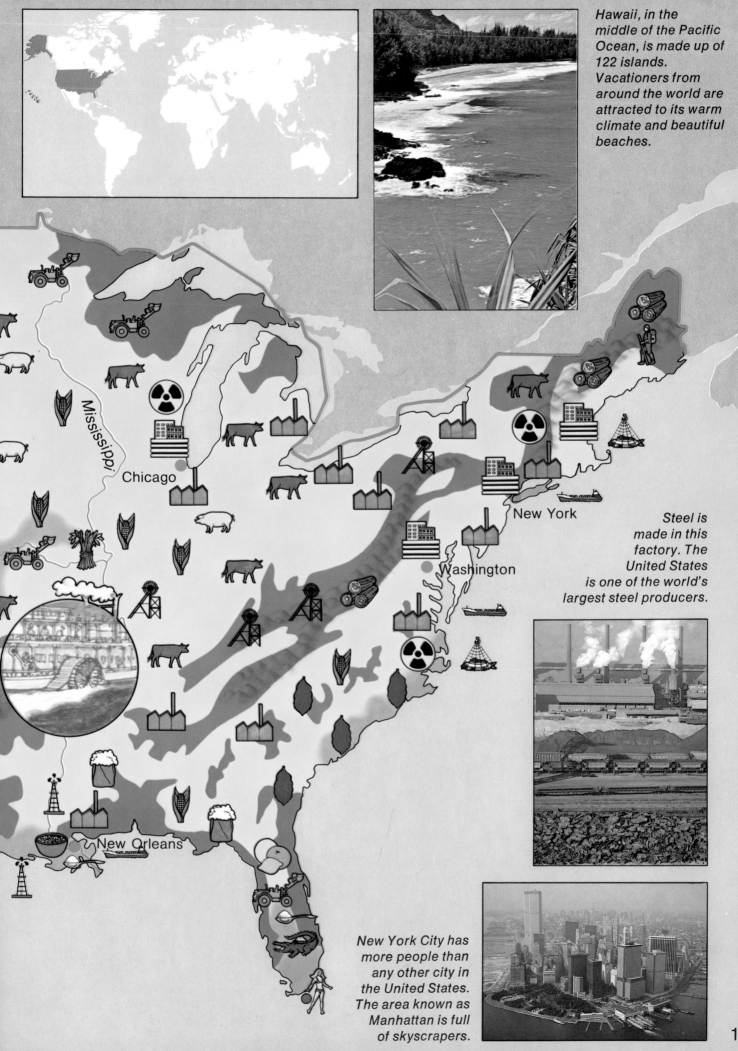

Hawaii, in the middle of the Pacific Ocean, is made up of 122 islands. Vacationers from around the world are attracted to its warm climate and beautiful beaches.

Mississippi

Chicago

New York

Washington

Steel is made in this factory. The United States is one of the world's largest steel producers.

New Orleans

New York City has more people than any other city in the United States. The area known as Manhattan is full of skyscrapers.

11

United States of America

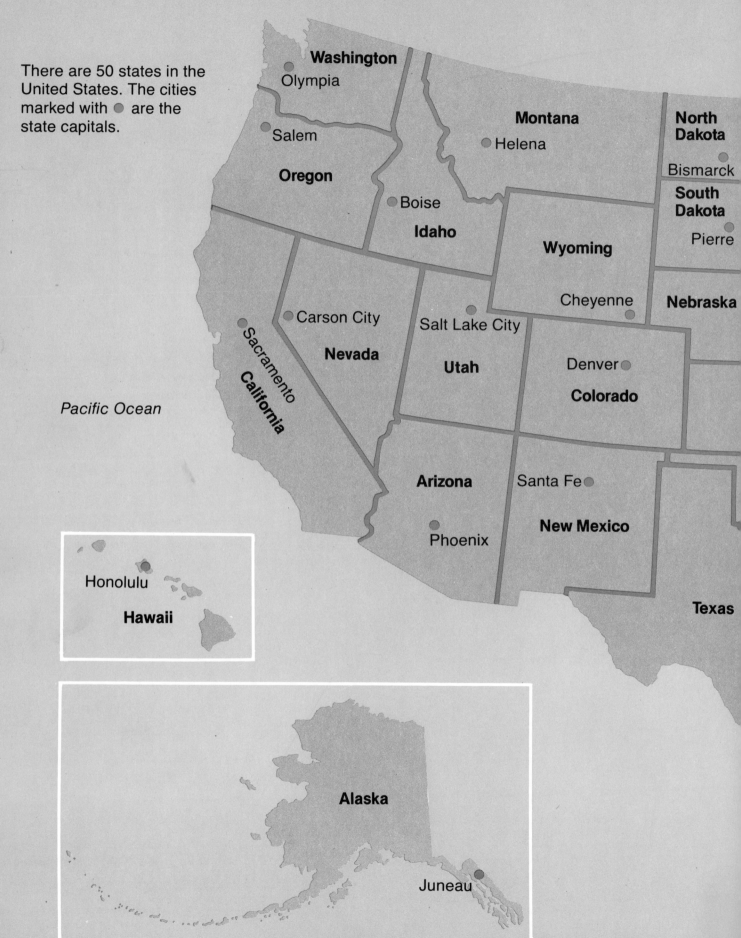

There are 50 states in the United States. The cities marked with ● are the state capitals.

Washington
Olympia

Salem

Oregon

Boise

Idaho

Montana
Helena

Wyoming

Cheyenne

North Dakota

Bismarck

South Dakota

Pierre

Nebraska

Carson City

Nevada

Sacramento

California

Pacific Ocean

Salt Lake City

Utah

Denver

Colorado

Arizona

Phoenix

Santa Fe

New Mexico

Honolulu

Hawaii

Texas

Alaska

Juneau

Minnesota

St. Paul

Wisconsin

Michigan

Madison

Lansing

Iowa

Des Moines

Illinois

Indiana

Ohio

Columbus

Lincoln

Springfield

Indianapolis

Missouri

Frankfort

Kentucky

West Virginia

Charleston

Richmond

Topeka

Jefferson City

Kansas

Virginia

North Carolina

Raleigh

Nashville

Oklahoma City

Arkansas

Tennessee

Columbia

Oklahoma

Little Rock

Mississippi

Alabama

Atlanta

Georgia

South Carolina

Louisiana

Montgomery

Austin

Jackson

Baton Rouge

Tallahassee

Florida

New Hampshire

Maine

Vermont

Augusta

Montpelier

Concord

Boston

Albany

Massachusetts

New York

Providence

Pennsylvania

Rhode Island

Harrisburg

Hartford

Connecticut

Trenton

New Jersey

Dover

Delaware

Annapolis

Maryland

Atlantic Ocean

Gulf of Mexico

13

Canada

There is tundra in northern Canada, in an area where it is too cold for trees to grow. In winter the land is covered with snow and ice. In the summer most of the ice melts and small plants grow everywhere in the wet ground. Not many people live in the tundra or the great forests. The cities and farms are further south where it is warmer.

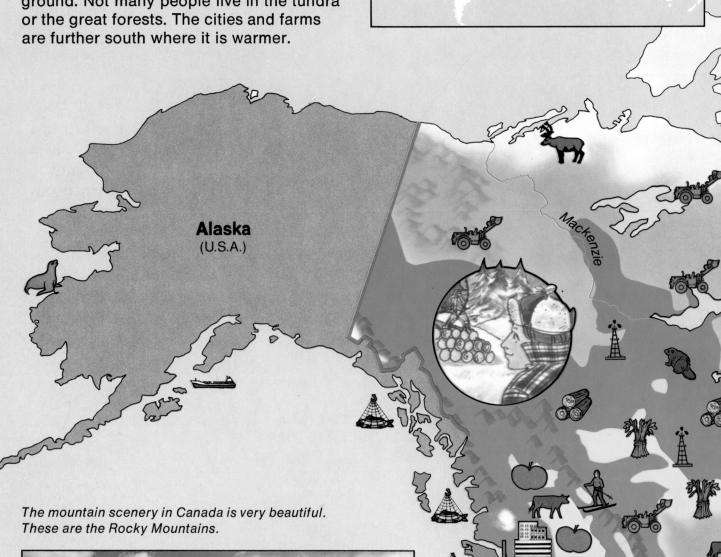

Alaska
(U.S.A.)

Mackenzie

Vancouver

The mountain scenery in Canada is very beautiful. These are the Rocky Mountains.

The man sawing the tree is called a lumberjack. The trees will be made into paper. Strong machines are used to lift the trees onto huge trucks and boats.

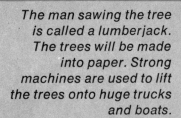

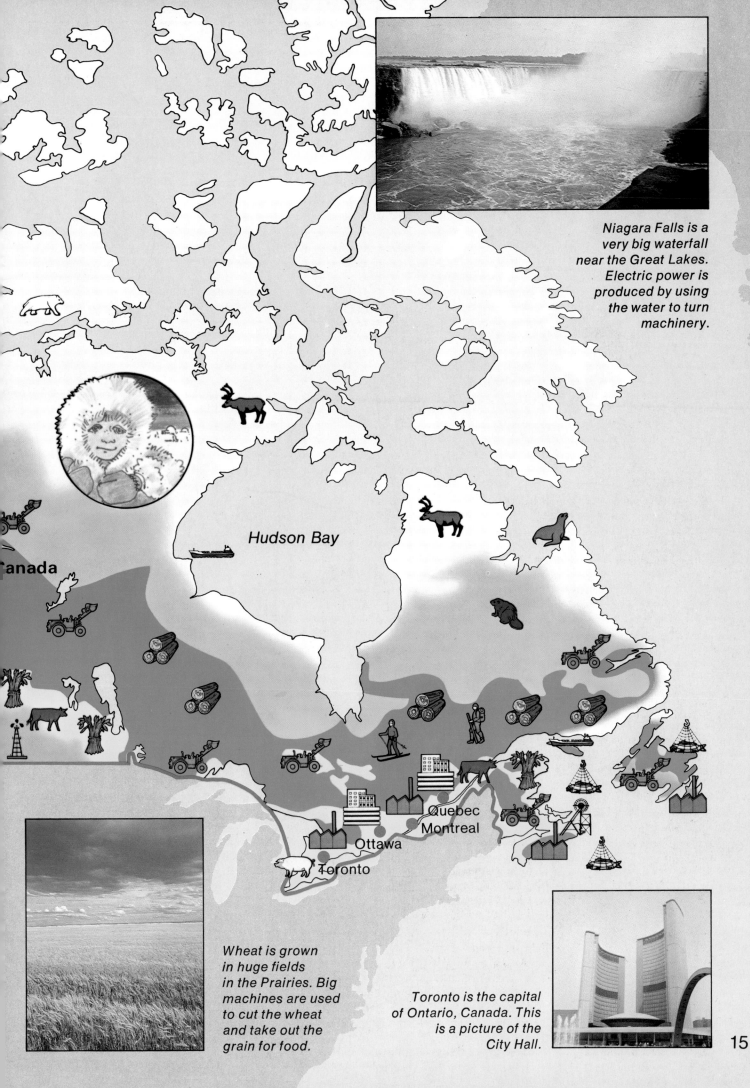

Niagara Falls is a very big waterfall near the Great Lakes. Electric power is produced by using the water to turn machinery.

Hudson Bay

Canada

Ottawa

Toronto

Quebec
Montreal

Wheat is grown in huge fields in the Prairies. Big machines are used to cut the wheat and take out the grain for food.

Toronto is the capital of Ontario, Canada. This is a picture of the City Hall.

15

Gulf and Caribbean Lands

In this area, there are high, dry mountains and wet, tropical jungles. Most people work on farms. Sugar cane and bananas are grown nearly everywhere. In the Caribbean Sea there are many tropical islands with palm trees along the shore. Brightly colored fish live around the coral reefs in the sea. Can you find the Panama Canal on the map? It is used by big ships to cross from one ocean to another.

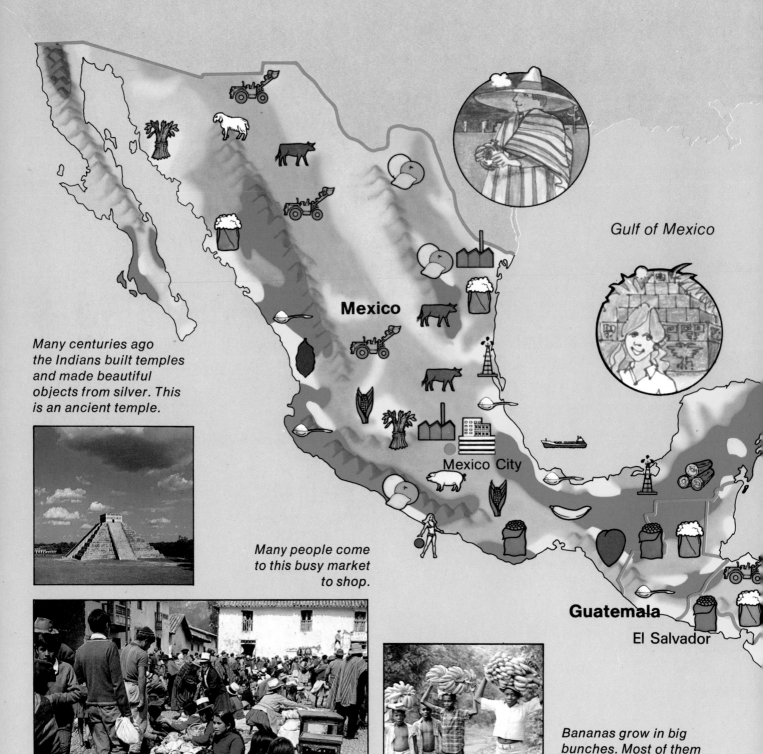

Gulf of Mexico

Mexico

Mexico City

Guatemala

El Salvador

Many centuries ago the Indians built temples and made beautiful objects from silver. This is an ancient temple.

Many people come to this busy market to shop.

Bananas grow in big bunches. Most of them are sold to other countries. When they are shipped they are green. They ripen to a bright yellow color while they travel.

16

This is the cane from which sugar is obtained.

Palm trees grow on this tropical island.

Some of the islands are famous for their steel bands. The people play drums made from oil drums, which give a very lively sound.

The Bahamas

Nassau

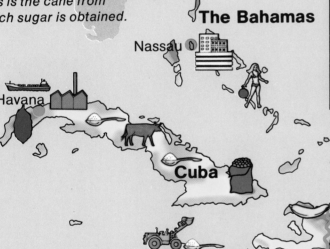

Havana

Cuba

Puerto Rico

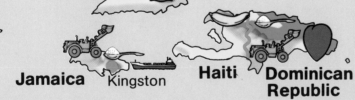

Jamaica   Kingston   **Haiti**   **Dominican Republic**

Honduras

Caribbean Sea

Barbados

Nicaragua

Trinidad

Costa Rica   Panama City

Panama Canal

South America

The inland part of Brazil is covered by a huge tropical forest. It rains nearly every day and the trees grow very tall and close together. Hardly any sunlight reaches the ground. Millions of plants and animals live in the rain forests. In South America there are some big farms whose owners are very wealthy. But most people are poor and have to work hard just to feed their families.

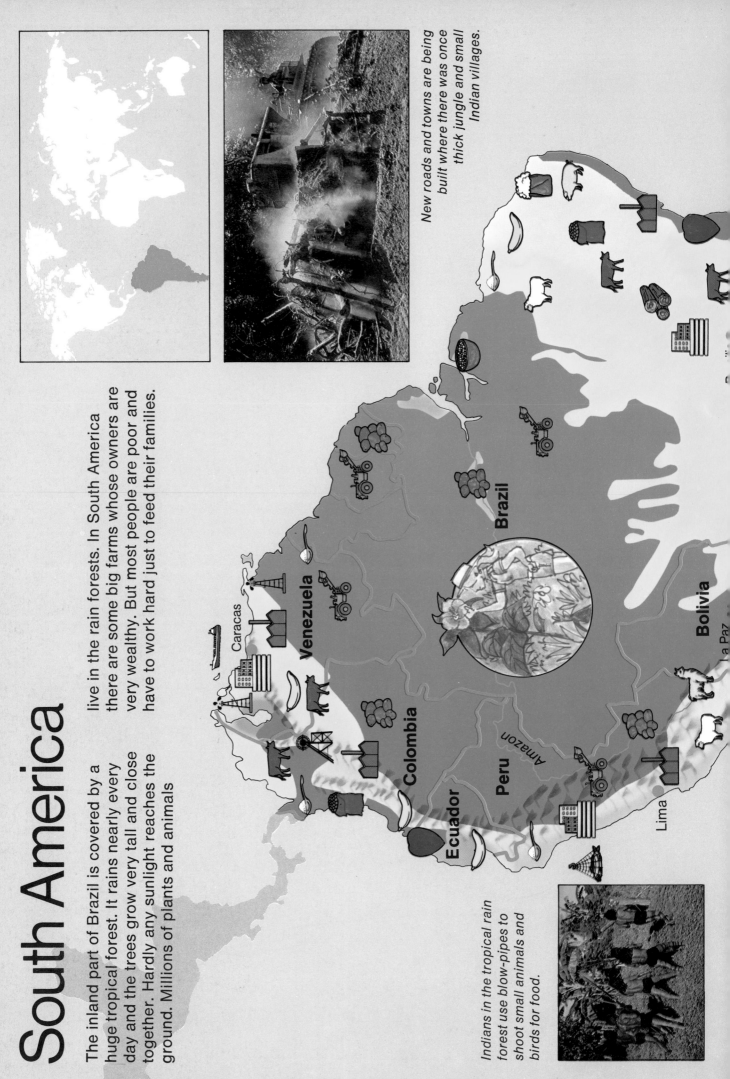

New roads and towns are being built where there was once thick jungle and small Indian villages.

Indians in the tropical rain forest use blow-pipes to shoot small animals and birds for food.

Caracas

Venezuela

Colombia

Ecuador

Peru

Amazon

Brazil

Bolivia

La Paz

Lima

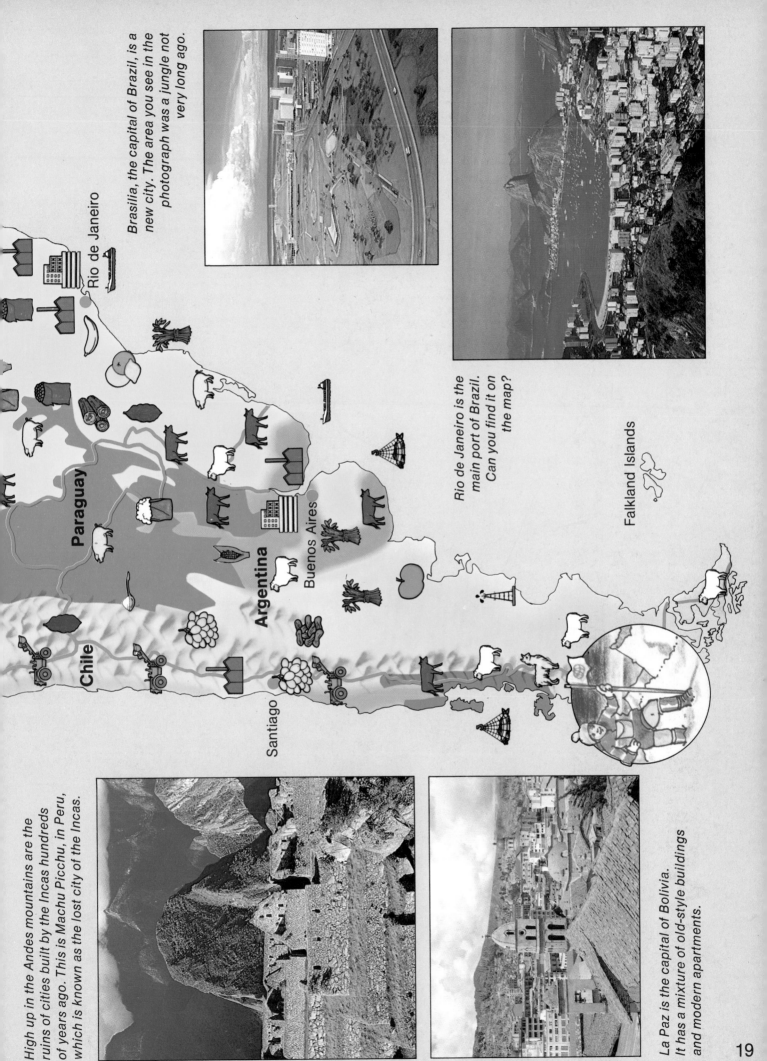

Brasilia, the capital of Brazil, is a new city. The area you see in the photograph was a jungle not very long ago.

Rio de Janeiro

Rio de Janeiro is the main port of Brazil. Can you find it on the map?

Falkland Islands

High up in the Andes mountains are the ruins of cities built by the Incas hundreds of years ago. This is Machu Picchu, in Peru, which is known as the lost city of the Incas.

La Paz is the capital of Bolivia. It has a mixture of old-style buildings and modern apartments.

Paraguay

Chile

Santiago

Argentina

Buenos Aires

Western Europe

There are many areas with lots of factories. Near the coast big steel works and oil refineries have been built, but in the mountains the factories are smaller. In Switzerland watches and clocks are made. The Swiss have become famous as manufacturers of good watches. Because the south of Europe is warm and sunny, grapes and other fruit can be grown. The coast of southern Europe is a popular vacation area.

Rotterdam is one of the biggest ports in the world.

People in Spain wear costumes like these for dancing and festivals.

North Sea

Netherlands

Rotterdam

Hamburg

Belgium

Brussels

West Germany

Rhine

Switzerland

Geneva

Austria

Vienna

Italy

Corsica

Rome

Sardinia

Sicily

Mediterranean Sea

Grapes are grown in vineyards in many parts of Western Europe. They are used to make different types of wine.

This German 'fairy tale' castle, was built in the last century.

This is a picture of the Matterhorn, a high mountain in the Alps.

Two thousand years ago the Romans had a very big empire. They built many cities. Many of the ruins can still be seen today. This one is the Colosseum in Rome.

This oil rig is supplying Britain with oil from under the North Sea.

Eastern Europe

The river shown on the map is the Danube. Boats travel along this river carrying goods to countries in Eastern and Western Europe.

In the cities of Eastern Europe there are many large factories and housing estates owned by the government. In the countryside some farmers live in villages which have not changed much for hundreds of years.

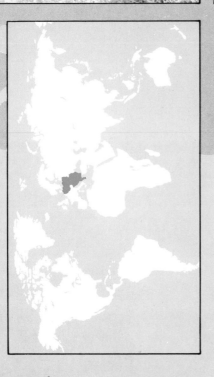

This farmer cuts wheat with a sickle.

This is a picture of Castle Cesky Krumlov in Czechoslovakia.

Christmas tree decorations are being made in this

Poland

Warsaw

Berlin

East Germany

Prague

Czechoslovakia

The Brandenburg Gate is in East Berlin, behind the

Black Sea

Danube

Romania

Bulgaria

Hungary

Belgrade

Yugoslavia

Dubrovnik

Albania

Greece

Athens

Crete

Mediterranean Sea

Places like Dubrovnik on the coast of Yugoslavia have become popular vacation areas.

These are the ruins of the Parthenon, a temple built by the Ancient Greeks.

Scandinavia

Most of the land is covered with forests, lakes, and mountains. In the North it is called "The Land of the Midnight Sun". This is because in summer the sun shines all through the night. In winter it is dark all through the day. The farmers in Denmark sell butter and bacon to other countries. The people in Sweden make paper from their trees for other countries. Most people live in the South, where there are farms, factories, and towns.

The Lapps look after herds of reindeer in the far North.

This is a picture of northern Scandinavia, "The Land of the Midnight Sun."

There are 66,000 lakes in Finland.

This steep-sided valley is called a fjord. There are fjords all along the coast of Norway.

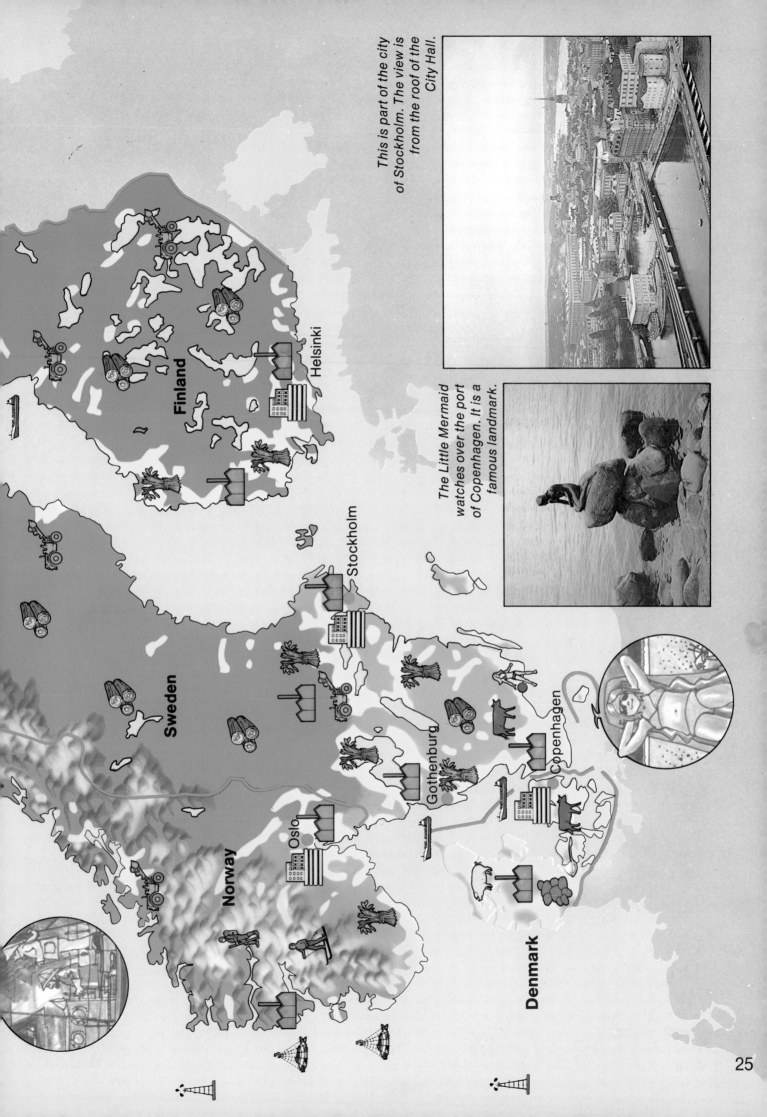

This is part of the city of Stockholm. The view is from the roof of the City Hall.

The Little Mermaid watches over the port of Copenhagen. It is a famous landmark.

Finland

Helsinki

Stockholm

Sweden

Norway

Oslo

Gothenburg

Copenhagen

Denmark

Soviet Union

The Soviet Union (Union of Soviet Social-ist Republics) is the biggest country in the world. Most people live in the western part where there are very large farms and factories. The government is trying to get more people to move to new towns in Siberia, the eastern part of the Soviet Union. The great forest is known as the Taiga. It is shaded green on the map. The forest stretches across the Soviet Union.

Leningrad

Moscow

Volga

Black Sea

Caspian Sea

This monastery is in Georgia, a province near the Black Sea.

At the Kosmos Centre in Moscow we can see how the people have used science to change and develop their lives.

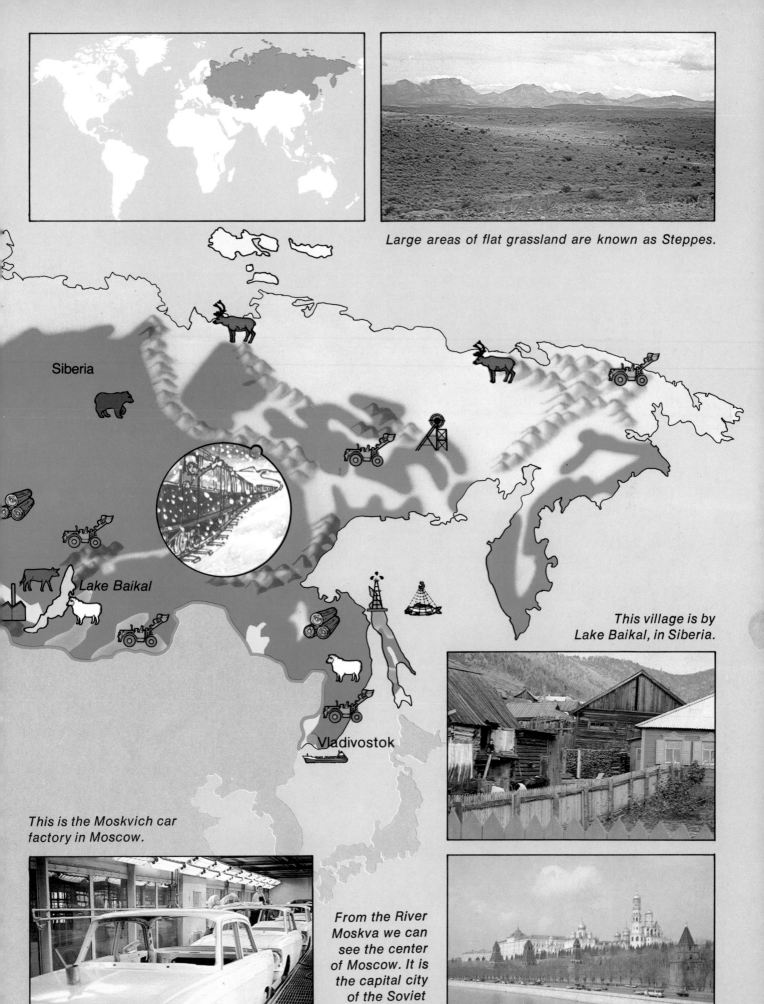

Large areas of flat grassland are known as Steppes.

Siberia

Lake Baikal

Vladivostok

This village is by
Lake Baikal, in Siberia.

This is the Moskvich car
factory in Moscow.

From the River
Moskva we can
see the center
of Moscow. It is
the capital city
of the Soviet
Union. We can
see its govern-
ment building,
the Kremlin.

Africa

There are many different countries in Africa. Some are big and others very small. Some countries are rich and others are poor. Most of them used to be ruled by people from other countries, such as Britain and France. Now they are ruled by their own people. The Sahara in North Africa is the largest dry area of land in the world. It is 5,000 kilometers from one end to the other.

In the desert there are some places where water can be found, often in small pools. Around these pools, plants and palm trees can grow.

Oil tankers and other big ships can go through the Suez Canal. This can make their journey shorter.

These elephants live in a special park in Uganda where they are protected from hunters. Can you find some wild animals on the map?

Suez
Cairo
Egypt
Nile
Sudan
Libya
Chad
Sahara
Niger
Tunisia
Algeria
Mali
Niger
Timbuktu
Mauritania
Casablanca
Morocco
Canary Islands

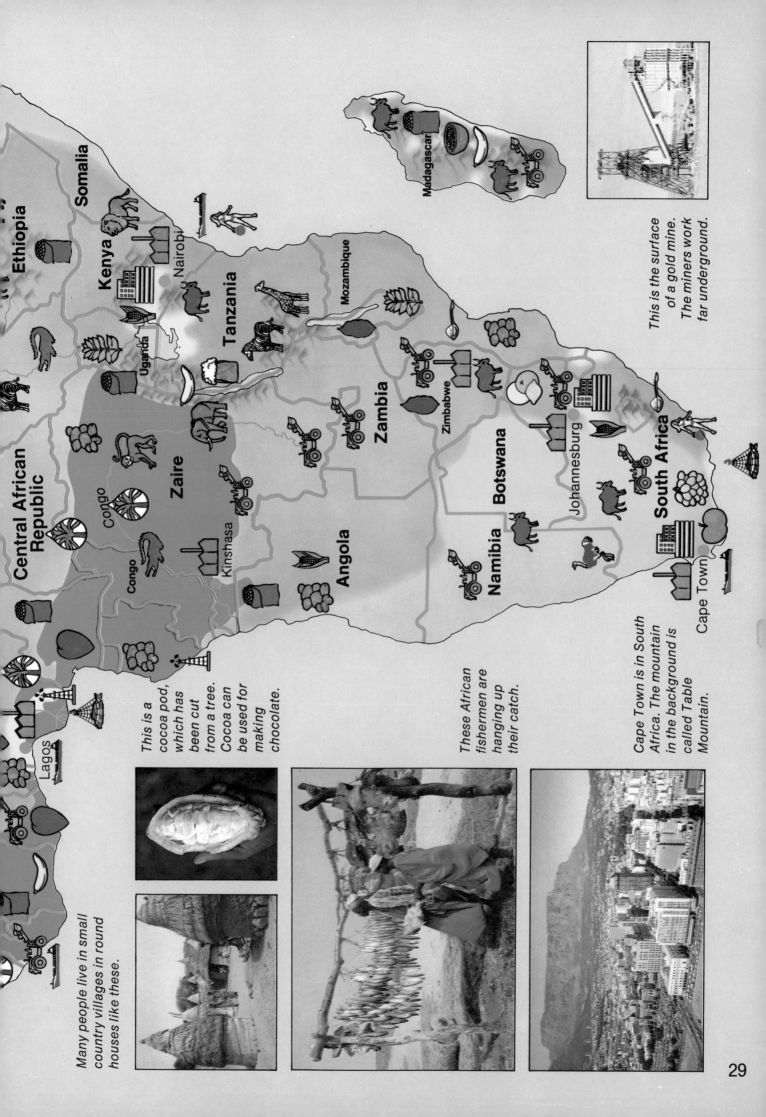

Ethiopia

Somalia

Kenya

Nairobi

Central African Republic

Uganda

Tanzania

Mozambique

Madagascar

Zaire

Congo

Congo

Kinshasa

Zambia

Zimbabwe

Angola

Namibia

Botswana

Johannesburg

Lagos

South Africa

Cape Town

This is the surface of a gold mine. The miners work far underground.

This is a cocoa pod, which has been cut from a tree. Cocoa can be used for making chocolate.

These African fishermen are hanging up their catch.

Cape Town is in South Africa. The mountain in the background is called Table Mountain.

Many people live in small country villages in round houses like these.

Middle East

A lot of the world's oil comes from the Middle East. Most of the land is very dry. In daytime it is hot, but at night it becomes cold. Some of the people who live in this area are nomads who travel in the desert with their camels. The Holy Cities of Jerusalem and Mecca are in the Middle East. Can you find them on the map?

Istanbul

Turkey

Cyprus

Lebanon

Mediterranean Sea

Israel
Jerusalem

Syria

Jordan

Red Sea

Sheepskin coats and rugs are for sale on this street in Jerusalem.

Onami tribesmen protect their heads from the fierce sun by wearing turbans.

These nomads live in sturdy tents that can protect them from the heat of the day and the cold of the night.

A rig is drilling for oil in Iran. To the right are the flames from waste gases that are being safely destroyed.

A Turkish peasant tends his flock of sheep.

Tehran

Iran

Baghdad

Iraq

Kuwait

Persian Gulf

Qatar

United Arab Emirates

Saudi Arabia

Mecca

Oman

South Yemen

Yemen

When filled with oil, this supertanker, belonging to the British Petroleum Company, weighs 250,000 tons.

South-West Asia

This is an area of high mountains and wide valleys. Can you find Mount Everest on the map? It is the highest place on earth.

For long periods there is no rain at all and the crops die. Sometimes there are terrible floods which destroy houses and farms. Many people do not have enough to eat. In the cities there are some modern factories and new buildings, as well as beautiful temples and old palaces. Most people can only afford to live in small, run-down houses.

The Taj Mahal was built by a great Prince. It is made of white marble.

Mount Everest is the highest mountain in the world.

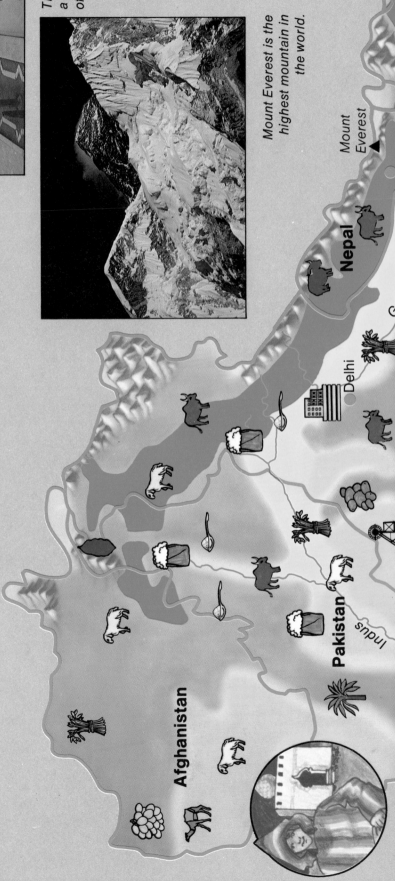

Afghanistan

Pakistan

Nepal

Delhi

Mount Everest

Indus

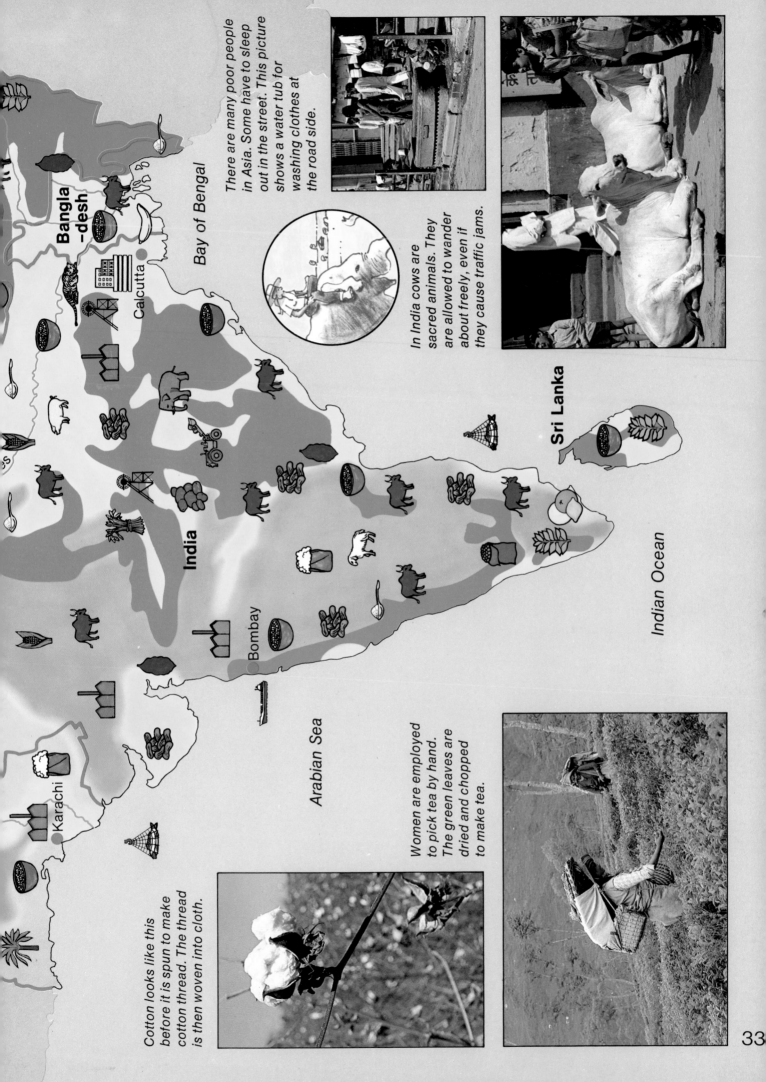

Bangla-desh

Bay of Bengal

Calcutta

There are many poor people in Asia. Some have to sleep out in the street. This picture shows a water tub for washing clothes at the road side.

In India cows are sacred animals. They are allowed to wander about freely, even if they cause traffic jams.

India

Bombay

Sri Lanka

Indian Ocean

Arabian Sea

Karachi

Women are employed to pick tea by hand. The green leaves are dried and chopped to make tea.

Cotton looks like this before it is spun to make cotton thread. The thread is then woven into cloth.

China and Its Neighbors

More people live in the People's Republic of China than in any other country in the world. Most of them live in the countryside and work together in the fields or in small factories. Rice is their main food. It needs a lot of water to grow, so the rivers are used to irrigate the fields.

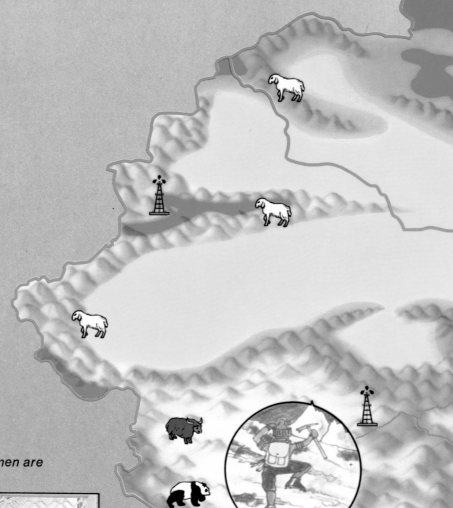

Mongolia

GREAT WALL

China

Hwa

These Chinese women are washing clothes.

These fields are flooded to grow rice. They are called paddy fields.

Many people work together to dig up rocks and to build dams that control the rivers.

In this school in China, the children are writing the Chinese alphabet.

Peking

Yangtze Kiang

Shanghai

North Korea

South Korea

Taiwan

Hong Kong

The Great Wall was built a very long time ago to protect the Chinese from their enemies.

This temple is in Peking, China.

Natural rubber comes from rubber trees. A cut is made in the bark and a cup tied on to collect the rubber.

The ancient temples of Thailand have changed very little. Here we can see young monks in their brightly colored robes.

Burma

Vietnam

Hanoi

Laos

Thailand

Bangkok

Cambodia
(Kampuchea)

Philippines

Manila

Hø Chi Minh

South China Sea

M a l a y s i a

Singapore

Singapore is one of the great ports of the East. People from many different lands live in this city.

I n d o n

Djakarta

Java

36

South-East Asia

Most of South-East Asia is covered with tropical rain forest. Hundreds of years ago, traders came from Europe and took back home precious oils and spices. They called these islands the East Indies. Today, there are many very big cities in South-East Asia. Millions of people leave the countryside and move to the cities to find jobs. Can you find the island of Java on the map? It is one of the most densely populated islands in the world.

The islands are crowded with people. Some of the people live in boats on the water. They buy food at floating markets like this one in the photograph.

Where the land is hilly, rice is grown on fields which are cut into the hillsides.

In the big cities, many of the poor people live in shanties. These are houses made of old scraps of wood and other things.

s   i   a

New Guinea

Japan

The Japanese factories make radios, calculators, automobiles, motor bikes, and toys. Japan also has a very large number of shipyards and builds more ships than any other country.

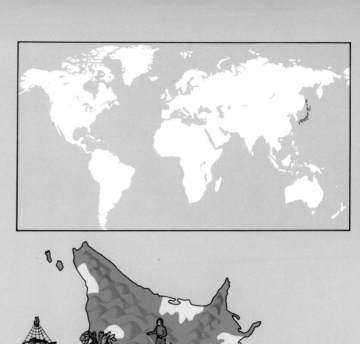

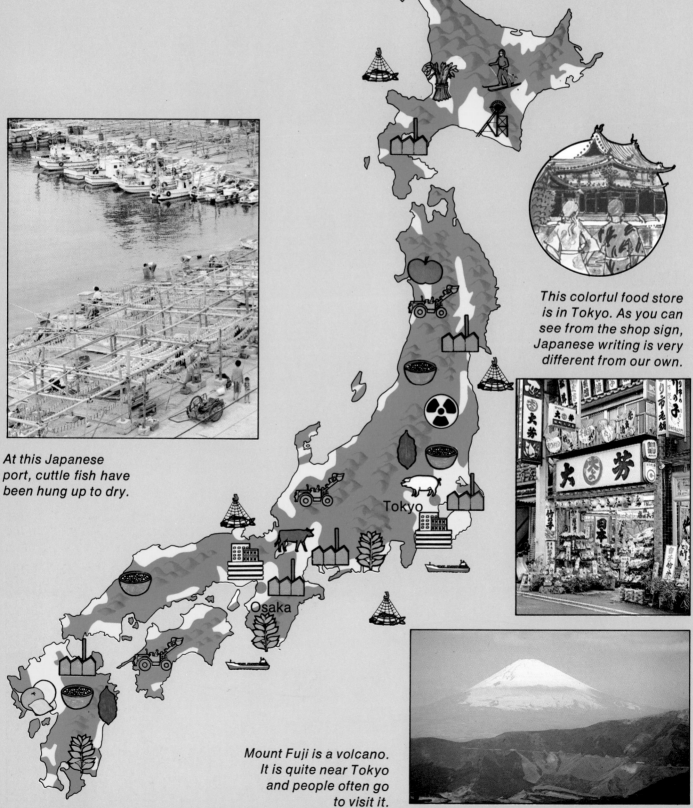

At this Japanese port, cuttle fish have been hung up to dry.

Tokyo

Osaka

This colorful food store is in Tokyo. As you can see from the shop sign, Japanese writing is very different from our own.

Mount Fuji is a volcano. It is quite near Tokyo and people often go to visit it.

New Zealand

New Zealand sends wool, meat, and butter to other countries. In the North Island there are volcanoes and geysers. A geyser is a hot water fountain.

These people are Maoris. Maoris lived in New Zealand long before European explorers discovered their country.
They used to wear clothes like this all the time, but now they only dress up for special occasions.

North Island

Auckland

Wellington

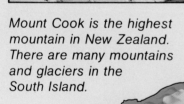

Mount Cook is the highest mountain in New Zealand. There are many mountains and glaciers in the South Island.

Christchurch

South Island

This is a geyser. The water is very hot, as you can see from the steam coming off it.

Australia

The first people in Australia were the Aborigines. Now they have land in only a few parts of Australia. Australia is a rich country. There are large farms and mines. Nearly all the people live in towns and cities on the coast. The middle of Australia is very dry and not many people live there.

Only a few Aborigines still appear like this. Most of them wear modern clothes and live in towns.

Perth

Wool from sheep is an important product of Australian farms.

Big new mines are being dug in Australia, far away from any cities. This one will provide ore for making iron.

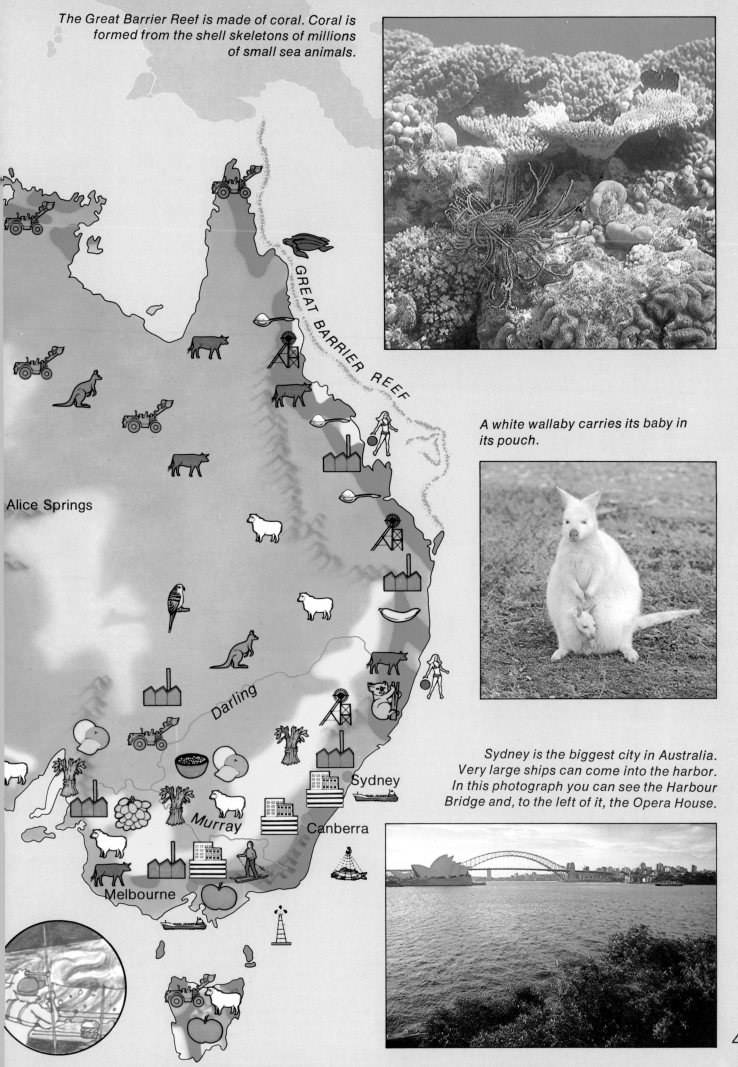

The Great Barrier Reef is made of coral. Coral is formed from the shell skeletons of millions of small sea animals.

A white wallaby carries its baby in its pouch.

Sydney is the biggest city in Australia. Very large ships can come into the harbor. In this photograph you can see the Harbour Bridge and, to the left of it, the Opera House.

GREAT BARRIER REEF

Alice Springs

Darling

Murray

Sydney

Canberra

Melbourne

North Polar Region

If Simon and Sarah were to get on a space-ship
and orbit the Earth, they would see that the Earth
is round. At the extreme northern end of the Earth
is the North Pole, where the sea is frozen to form
a solid ice cap.

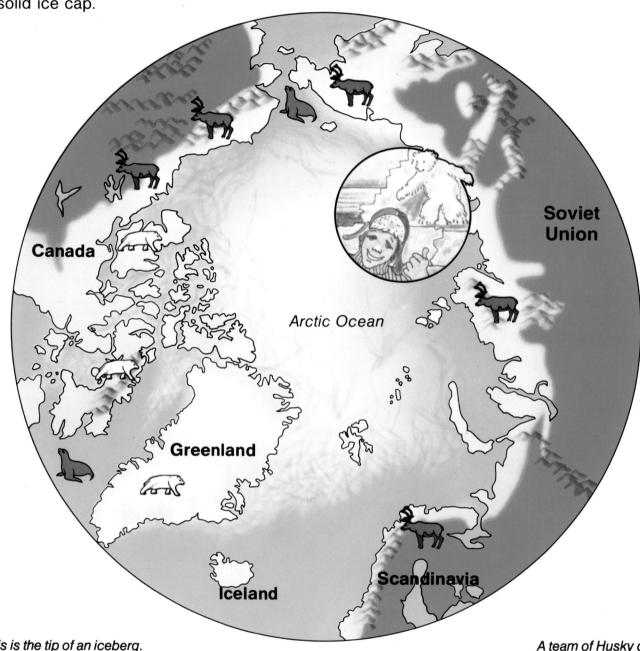

Soviet
Union

Canada

Arctic Ocean

Greenland

Iceland

Scandinavia

This is the tip of an iceberg.
Most of it floats under the cold water.

A team of Husky dogs
pulls travellers over snow and ice.

South Polar Region

At the other end of the Earth, Simon and Sarah would look down from their spaceship and see the South Pole and the frozen continent of Antarctica.

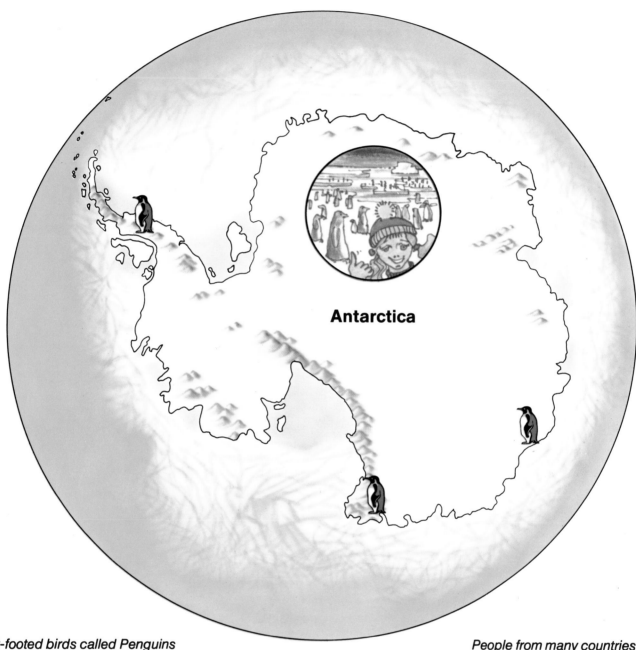

Antarctica

Flat-footed birds called Penguins have their home at the South Pole.

People from many countries visit Antarctica to carry out scientific work.

The World from Space

Looking at the world from space, Simon and Sarah would see the continents partly covered by clouds, as in this photograph taken by a satellite going around the Earth. Can you see which part of the world is shown on the photograph? The area of the Earth which is turned away from the sun is in darkness. The world spins round in space every day and there is always one half of our planet where it is night, and one half where it is day.

The planets and the Earth move around the sun.

MERCURY

VENUS

EARTH

MARS

JUPITER

SATURN

URANUS

NEPTUNE

PLUTO

MOON

As the Earth travels through space around the Sun, so the Moon travels around the Earth.

The Ages of Life on Earth

100 million years ago

200 million years ago

300 million years ago

400 million years ago

500 million years ago

The fourth age of life on earth

Some scientists have found signs of man dating back over 1 million years.

The third age of life on earth

From about 65 million years ago, the modern animals began to appear.

Giant Sloth

Mammoth

Hipparion

Sabre toothed Tiger

The second age of life on earth

Ended about 65 million years ago.

Rhamphorhynchus

Stegosaurus

Tyrannosaurus

The first age of life on earth

About 500 million years ago.

Squid

Trilobite

Fish

Winged Insects

Shellfish

Notes to Parents and Teachers

The educational aims of this book have been carefully considered. We seek to lead children from their familiar local environments, through the concept of maps of the continents, and on to the idea of the world as a planet in space. The maps are a general, introductory presentation of major countries, cities, and bodies of water.

We have tried to make the book as self-explanatory as possible, but some words and concepts may need further elaboration.